For Miro

Books by Marcus Pfister

THE RAINBOW FISH*
RAINBOW FISH TO THE RESCUE!*
THE CHRISTMAS STAR*
DAZZLE THE DINOSAUR*
I SEE THE MOON
PENGUIN PETE*
PENGUIN PETE'S NEW FRIENDS*
PENGUIN PETE AND PAT
PENGUIN PETE AND LITTLE TIM
PENGUIN PETE, AHOY!
HOPPER*
HOPPER HUNTS FOR SPRING
HOPPER'S EASTER SURPRISE
HANG ON, HOPPER!
HOPPER'S TREETOP ADVENTURE
WAKE UP, SANTA CLAUS!

*also available in Spanish

Copyright © 1997 by Nord-Süd Verlag AG, Gossau Zürich, Switzerland.
First published in Switzerland under the title Mats und die Felsmäuse.
English translation copyright © 1997 by North-South Books Inc.
All rights reserved.
No part of this book may be reproduced or utilized in any form
or by any means, electronic or mechanical, including photocopying,
recording, or any information storage and retrieval system,
without permission in writing from the publisher.

First published in the United States, Great Britain, Canada,
Australia, and New Zealand in 1997 by North-South Books,
an imprint of Nord-Süd Verlag AG, Gossau Zürich, Switzerland.
Distributed in the United States by North-South Books Inc., New York.

Library of Congress Cataloging-in-Publication Data is available.
A CIP catalogue record for this book is available from The British Library.
ISBN 1-55858-682-2 (trade binding)
1 3 5 7 9 TB 10 8 6 4 2
Printed in Belgium

For more information about our books, and the authors and artists
who create them, visit our web site: http://www.northsouth.com

Milo and the Magical Stones

Written and Illustrated by Marcus Pfister

Translated by Marianne Martens

North-South Books
New York · London

In the middle of the sea there was an island, and on this
island lived Milo and the other cliff mice. They loved their island.
It provided them with food and shelter and protection from
the rough storms that pounded waves against the cliffs.

During the summer Milo and his friends worked hard gathering food. Sometimes they would take a break from their work and skip flat stones out over the sea.

In the evenings the mice would stretch out on the cliffs that had been warmed by the sun, and watch the stars in the night sky. If it was warm enough, they would spend the entire night outside telling stories and enjoying the mild summer air.

But when the first winter storms arrived, the mice would spend most of the time huddled in their dark, damp caves, dreaming of light and warmth.

After one of these storms Milo crept out of his cave looking for
food. He poked his nose curiously into every crevice. Then, in
a particularly deep crevice, he saw something extraordinary—a
strange glowing stone! Using a long stick, he carefully pried it out
and carried it back to his cave.

Milo was amazed to see that the darker it got, the more brightly the stone glowed, and not only did it provide light, it also gave off a comforting warmth. Happily Milo curled up in the corner of his cave with his treasure. But he was not alone for long, because the bright light soon attracted the other mice.

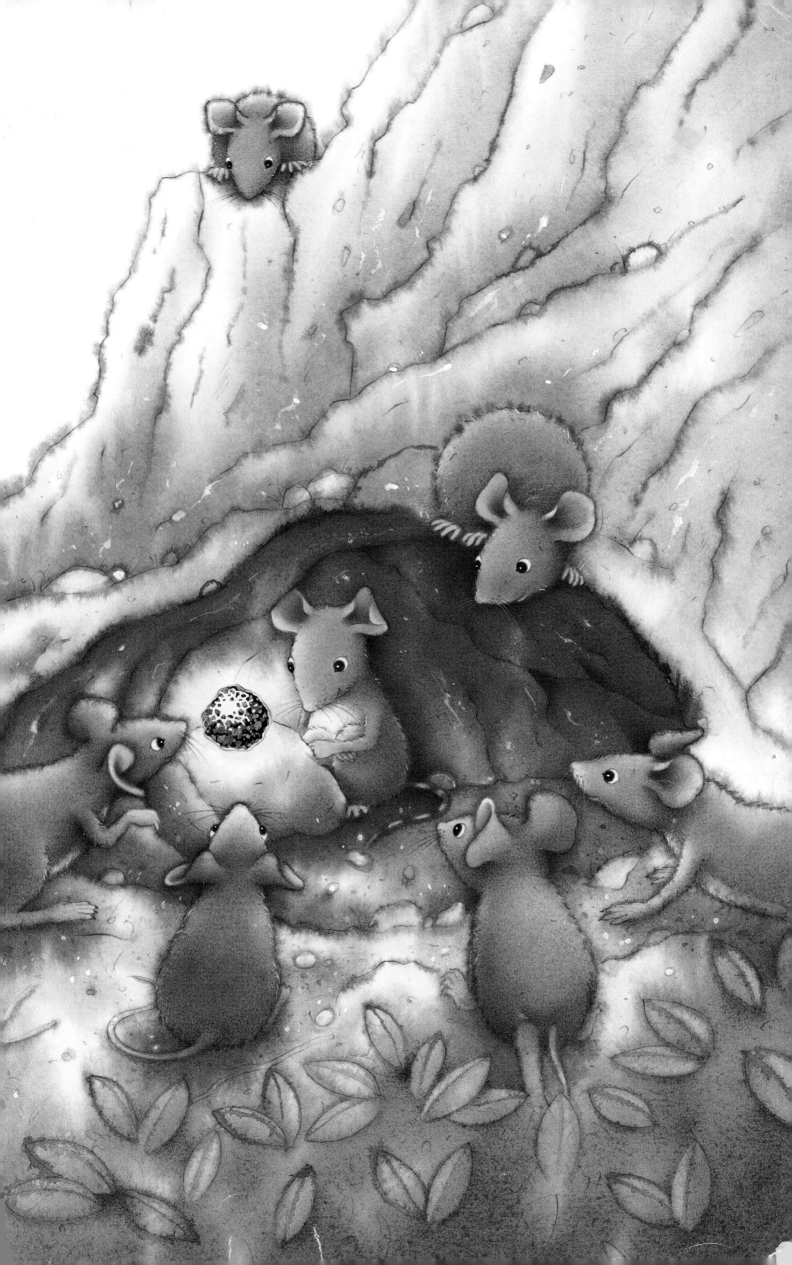

Everyone wanted a stone of his own, and they asked Milo to show them where he had found his. But just as they were about to set off, wise Balthazar stood up and spoke. "Don't forget," he said. "The stones belong to the island. If you take something from the island, you must give something in return."

THE HAPPY ENDING

"Balthazar is right," said Milo.

But what could Milo give to the island? He thought about it for many days, until at last he had an idea. He went down to the shore where the sea washed up all kinds of stones, and looked for one that was about the same size as the one he had taken.

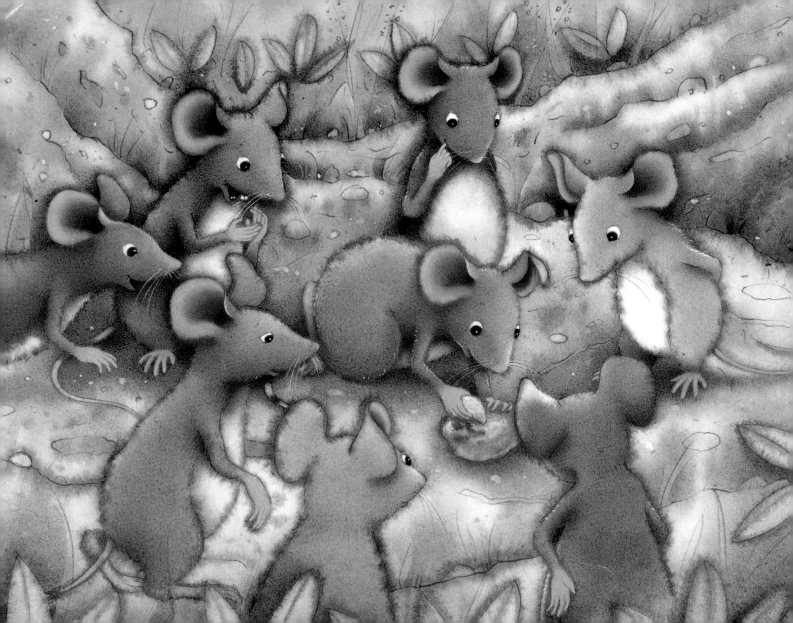

He sat down and started chipping away at the stone. Curious, the other mice gathered around. Milo worked for hours, until he had carved a beautiful sun into the stone. Then Milo led his friends to the hidden crevice in the mountain and put his carved stone in the place where he had found the glowing stone.

The other mice began digging. Directly below the crevice, they found a tunnel that ran deep into the mountain. The further into the mountain they went, the more glowing stones they found. Each mouse took one and carefully carried it home.

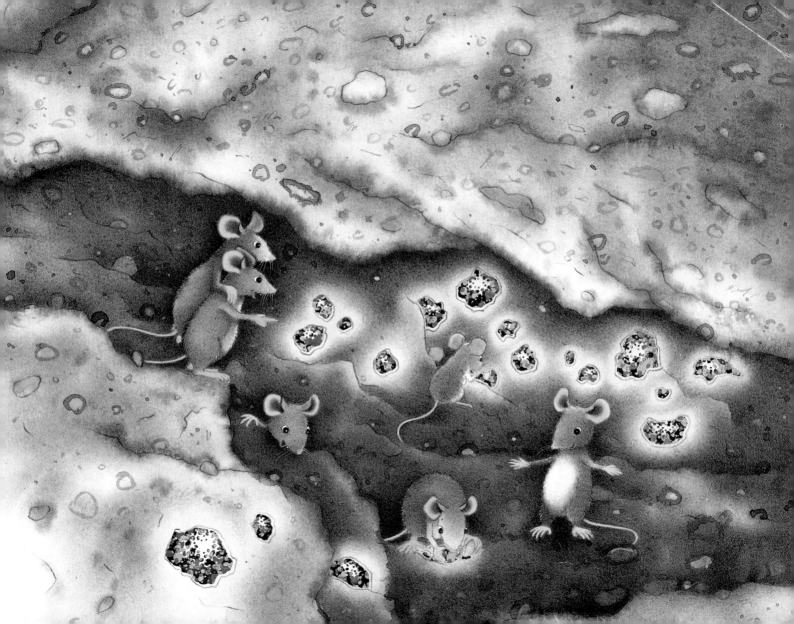

Then, like Milo, they found ordinary stones along the shore and started to decorate them. Some mice carved, etched, or drew on their stones. Others wrapped them or decorated them with flowers, leaves, or roots. They created beautiful works of art, then carried them deep into the mountain and placed their gifts where they had found the glowing stones.

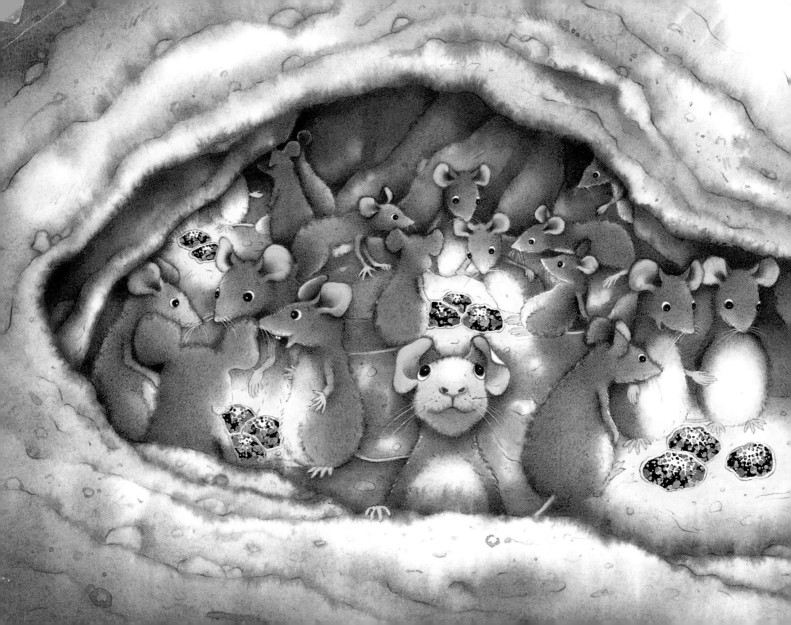

From then on the windy winter weather did not bother
the mice, who snuggled happily in their bright, warm caves.
Often they got together and told stories—just like they did
in the summertime. These gatherings made the long, cold
nights seem shorter and winter less damp and dark.

Every year the mice celebrated the beginning of winter. They met in Balthazar's cave and danced and sang. When it got dark, they took the magical stones on a parade along the cliffs as a special tribute to their beloved island.

THE SAD ENDING

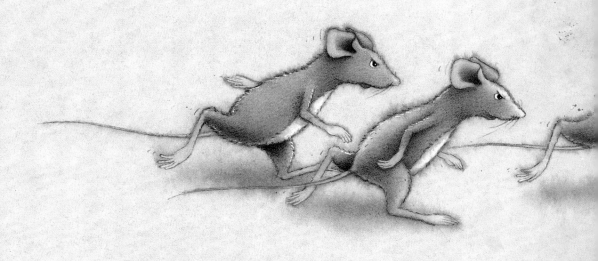

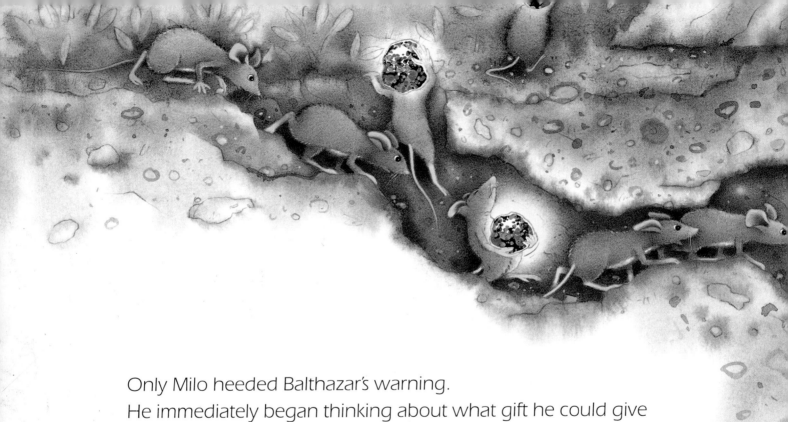

Only Milo heeded Balthazar's warning.

He immediately began thinking about what gift he could give to the island. But the other mice hurried off to find the glowing stones. They squeezed into the tunnel and started digging wildly. Using sharp rocks, they chipped away at the walls of the tunnel. They tossed the smaller stones aside—they wanted only the biggest ones.

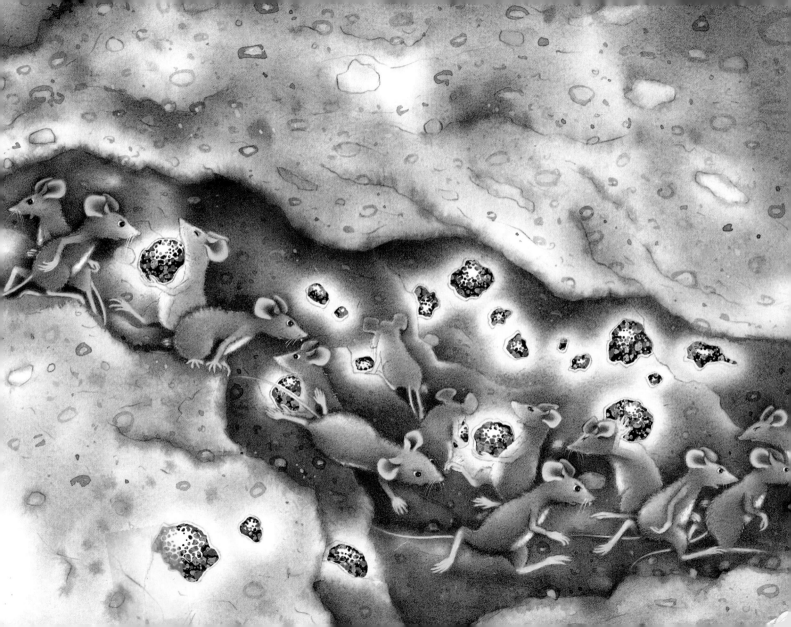

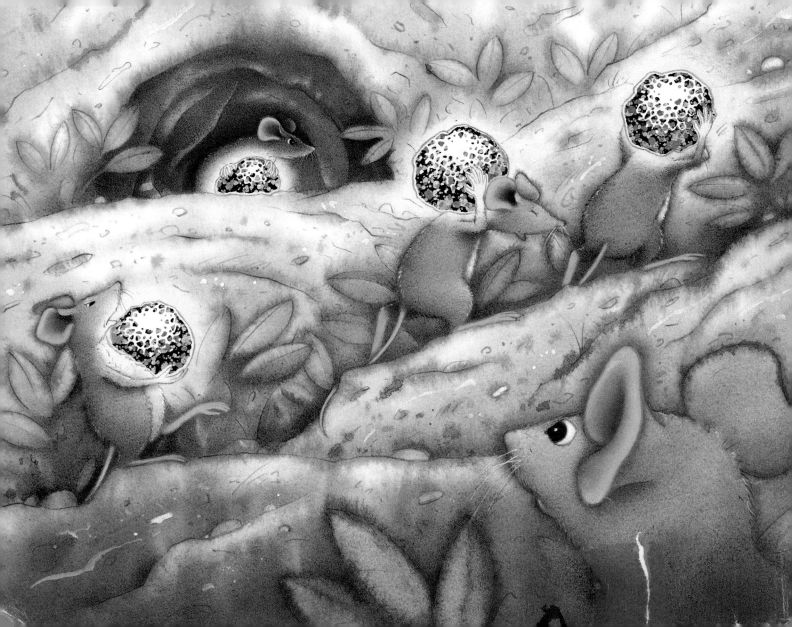

Then the mice dragged the glowing stones into their caves. They grew greedy and jealous, and spent so much time worrying about who had the most stones that they couldn't even enjoy the comfort the stones brought to them.

Milo watched his friends sadly. He worried about what Balthazar had said, and wondered what would happen. He sighed. There was nothing he could do but get back to work on the gift he had thought of to give to the island.

Soon the mice decided that they needed more of the magical stones. They crept back into the tunnel and dug day and night, piling the magical stones in and around their caves, until the whole island glowed. They boasted about their stones, and argued about who had the most, the biggest, the brightest.

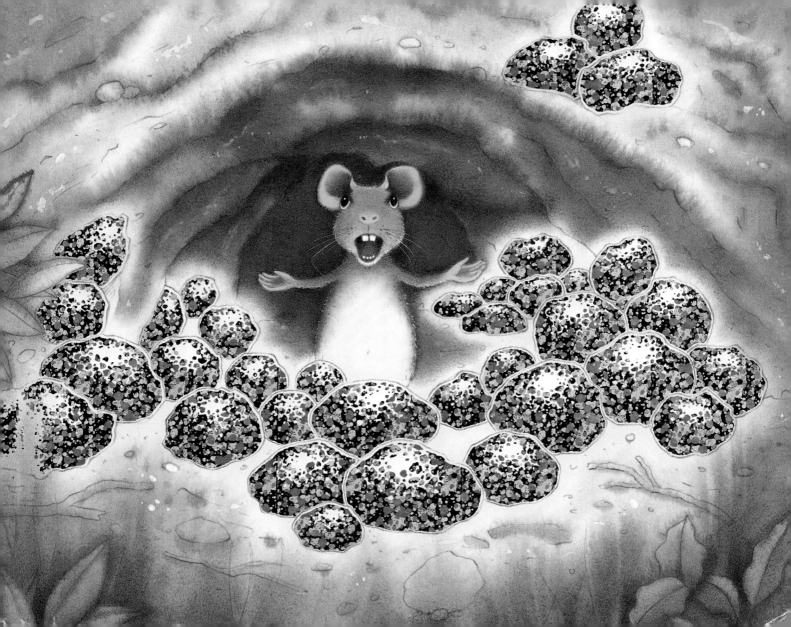

The mice were consumed with greed, and as they dug deeper and deeper, the walls of the mountain got thinner and thinner. Before long the mountain was hollowed out completely.

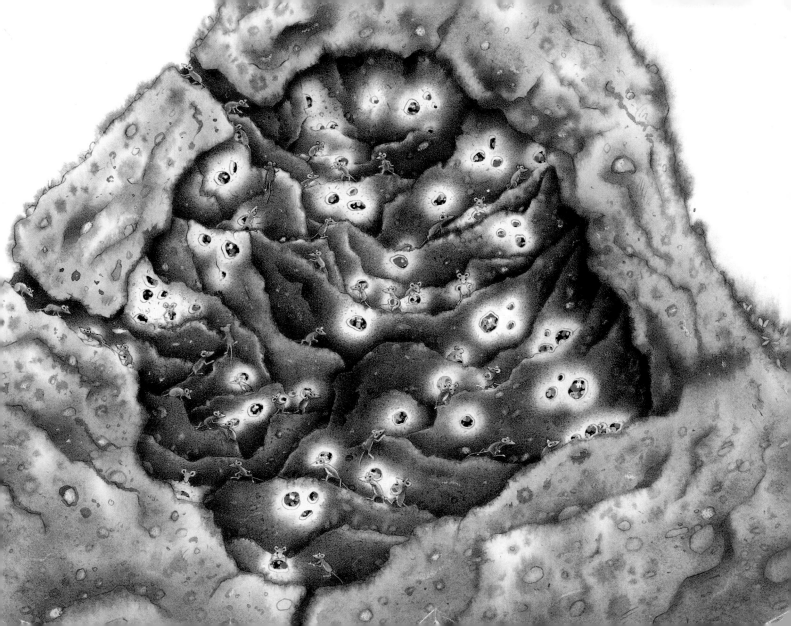

Then suddenly, with a thunderous roar, the mountain collapsed! Giant boulders fell, burying the tunnels in a heap of rubble. Waves pounded against the shore, flooding most of the island.

Only one cave was left. Inside, Milo and Balthazar crouched trembling in a corner.

"The stones could have brought such happiness," said Balthazar quietly. As he spoke, Milo went back to work, carving a stone to give to the island in thanks for its magical gift.

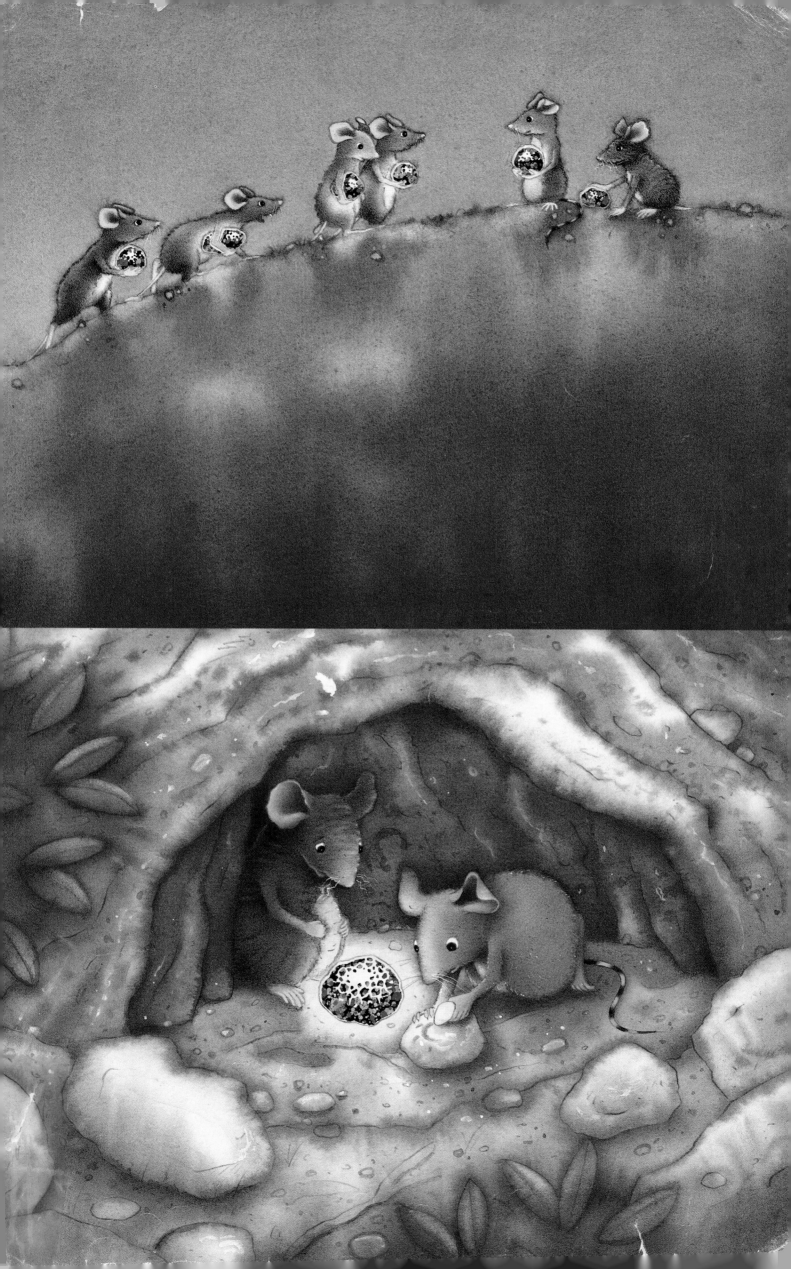

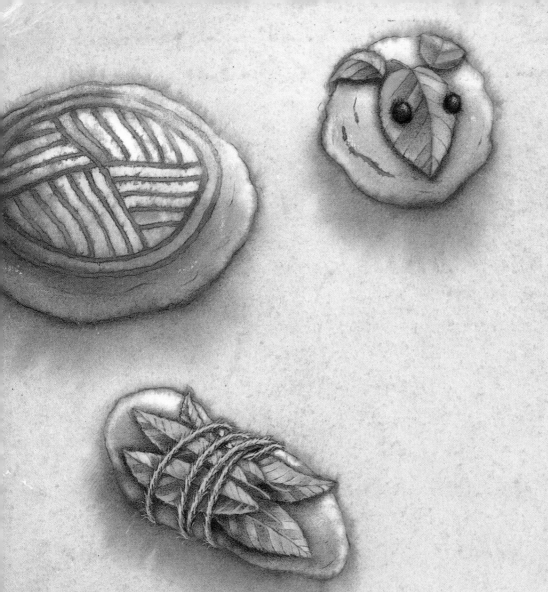
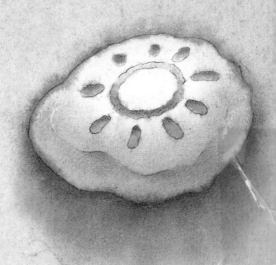